1 84121 240 7

1 84121 238 5

1 84121 248 2

1 84121 256 3

1 84121 236 9

1 84121 246 6

1 84121 230 X

1 84121 234 2

1 84121 254 7

Stella's Staying Put

The Most Stubborn Swan in the World!

Rose Impey
Shoo Rayner

ORCHARD BOOKS

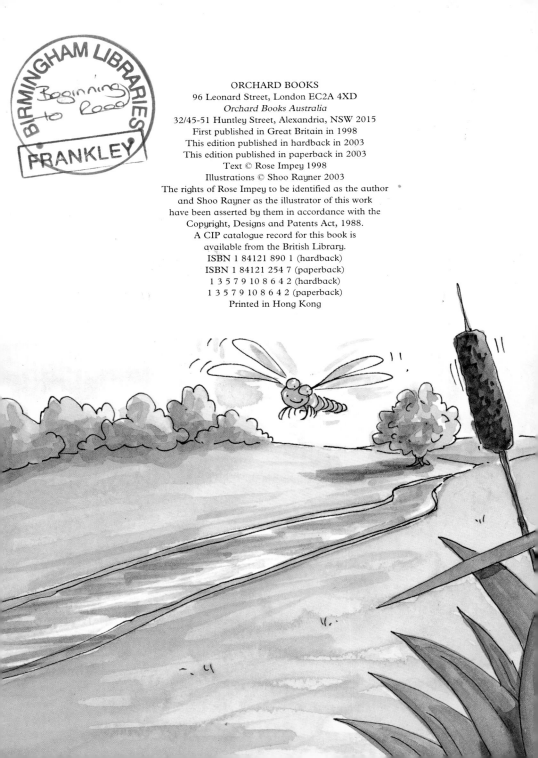

ORCHARD BOOKS
96 Leonard Street, London EC2A 4XD
Orchard Books Australia
32/45-51 Huntley Street, Alexandria, NSW 2015
First published in Great Britain in 1998
This edition published in hardback in 2003
This edition published in paperback in 2003
Text © Rose Impey 1998
Illustrations © Shoo Rayner 2003
The rights of Rose Impey to be identified as the author
and Shoo Rayner as the illustrator of this work
have been asserted by them in accordance with the
Copyright, Designs and Patents Act, 1988.
A CIP catalogue record for this book is
available from the British Library.
ISBN 1 84121 890 1 (hardback)
ISBN 1 84121 254 7 (paperback)
1 3 5 7 9 10 8 6 4 2 (hardback)
1 3 5 7 9 10 8 6 4 2 (paperback)
Printed in Hong Kong

Stella's Staying Put

Stella was a silly swan.
In fact she was a *stupid* swan.
But worse than that,
Stella was a very stubborn swan.

From the moment she was born,
Stella was determined to do things
her way.

"This way," said their mother.
Susie followed
and Shula followed,
but Stella went her own way.

9

"Watch me," said their father.

Susie did it like Dad
and Shula did it like Dad.

But Stella did
back flips

and belly flops

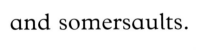

and somersaults.

Stella liked to do everything
her own way.

And when Stella got hold
of something, she wouldn't let it go.
Stella was the most stubborn swan
in the world.

Her parents shook their heads.
"Stella likes to be different," they said.
"She'll probably grow out of it."
But she didn't.
In fact, Stella got worse.

When the three swan sisters grew up,
they each looked for a mate.
Susie found Sammy.

Shula found Shep.

But Stella couldn't find anyone.
No one wanted Stella,
except Stan.

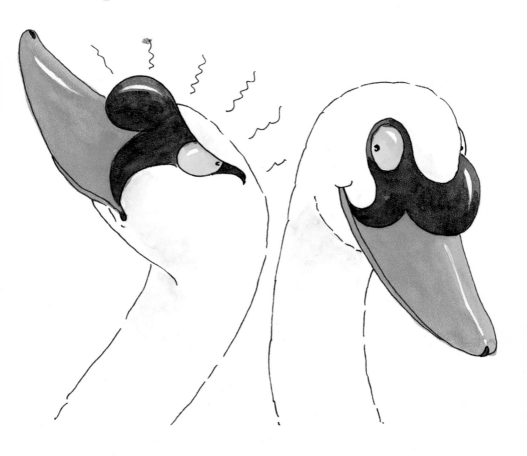

Stan was kind and loyal,
and very easy-going,
which was lucky for Stella.

The young swans all looked for
the best places to build their nests.
Susie and Sammy built their nest
on the smarter side of the river.

Shula and Shep built their nest
on a quiet little island,
where no one could reach them.
But Stan couldn't find any place
which would please Stella.

In the end, Stella sat down slap-bang in the middle of the towpath and started to build her nest there.

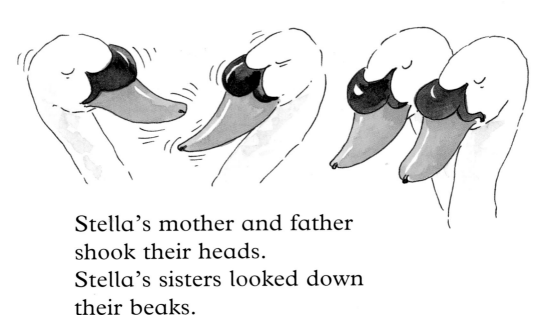

Stella's mother and father
shook their heads.
Stella's sisters looked down
their beaks.
But Stan just shrugged
and collected more twigs.
Stan was very loyal.

When their nests were finished,
the swan sisters laid their eggs
and sat on them.
Sammy swam to and fro
keeping Susie company.
Shep brought Shula
tasty things to eat.
They had a very easy life.

But life wasn't easy for Stan and Stella.
It was a struggle.
There was so much traffic,
it was like living in the middle
of a motorway.

Early each morning, fishermen
came past, in their big black boots.
"Sssss. Sssss," hissed Stan.
But the fishermen waved their
nets and rods at him.
They weren't afraid of a swan.

Canal boats came past
pulled by big brown horses
with huge hairy feet.

"Sssss. Sssss," hissed Stan.
But the horses plodded on,
pulling the boats behind them.
They weren't afraid of a swan.

People came past on their way
to work, or to walk their dogs.
Stan hissed and flapped
and almost wore himself out.

"We should move," he told Stella.

But it was too late to move.
The eggs were nearly ready to hatch.

"I'm not leaving my nest," said Stella.

I'm staying put.

Stan shrugged. What could he do?
He was determined to stick by Stella,
even if she was stubborn.

The days were hard but
the nights were even harder.
When it was dark, vandals from
the village came along,
trying to steal Stella's eggs.
Stan flapped his huge wings
and chased them away.

One night he chased them
across two fields, all the way
back to the village.

Stan was scared and exhausted.
But he still kept going, until
finally he realised he was lost.
He couldn't find his way home.

Stan lay down to rest.
He thought about Stella,
sitting on her eggs in the dark,
waiting for him.

"He'll soon be back," she told herself.
But Stan didn't come back
that night or the next.

Now when people came too close,
there was no one to chase them away.
Stella had to hiss and flap her own wings.
She was on and off her eggs all day long.
Soon she was worn out.
And hungry too.

Stella sent a message to her sisters asking for help.

"Oh no," said Susie. "Sammy's far too busy."

"I'm sorry," said Shula. "Shep has his own family to look after."

Stella's sisters thought that it served her right.

"Perhaps this will teach her not to be so stubborn," they said.

Poor Stella didn't know what to do.
Her eggs were about to hatch
and she couldn't leave them.
Now Stella *had* to stay put.

That night, a fox came by.
The fox was after Stella's eggs too.
He watched Stella with his sharp eyes.
And Stella watched him.
She was very scared but she
didn't move.

The fox came close.
He thought Stella would run away,
but Stella wasn't running anywhere.

Stella knew she'd been a silly swan.
She knew she'd been a stupid swan.
But she was also a stubborn swan
and Stella was staying put.

Suddenly, the fox came even closer.
He opened his mouth in a grin.
Stella could see his sharp teeth.
She stretched up to her full height
and gave the most horrible hiss
in the world.

SSSSs!

The fox backed off.
Stella wouldn't give in,
but neither would the fox.

He kept
coming back,

all through
the night.

Just when Stella felt too weak
to even open her beak,
she heard the sound of hissing.

The fox turned and saw Stan.
The fox might be a match
for one swan, but not for two.
Stella and Stan soon saw him off.

Stan settled down beside Stella
and tucked in his wings.
"You were very brave," he told her.
"But next time, let's choose
a quieter spot."

Stella, the most stubborn swan
in the world, said, "Maybe."
She was too tired to be stubborn –
just now.

Crack-A-Joke

How do monsters
like their eggs?
Terrifried!

What did the eggs say
in the monastery?
**Oh well, out of the
frying pan and into the friar!**

How do you get down from a horse?
You don't. You get down from a swan.

That's an
egg-stremely
bad joke!

What is white and yellow and goes at 90 kilometres an hour?
A train driver's egg sandwich!

Did you hear about the bad egg?
He got egg-spelled!

Waiter, this egg is rotten!

Don't blame me, madam. I only laid the table.

There are 16 Colour Crackers books.
Collect them all!

Colour Crackers are available from all good bookshops,
or can be ordered direct from the publisher:
Orchard Books, PO BOX 29, Douglas IM99 1BQ
Credit card orders please telephone 01624 836000 or fax 01624 837033
or e-mail: bookshop@enterprise.net for details.
To order please quote title, author and ISBN and your full name and address.
Cheques and postal orders should be made payable to 'Bookpost plc'.
Postage and packing is FREE within the UK
(overseas customers should add £1.00 per book).
Prices and availability are subject to change.

A Medal for **Poppy**
The Pluckiest Pig in the World!
Rose Impey and Shoo Rayner

1 84121 244 X

Tiny Tim
The Longest-Jumping Frog in the World!
Rose Impey and Shoo Rayner

1 84121 240 7

Sleepy **Sammy**
The Sleepiest Sloth in the World!
Rose Impey and Shoo Rayner

1 84121 238 5

Rhode Island **Roy**
The Roughest Rooster in the World!
Rose Impey and Shoo Rayner

1 84121 252 0

We Want **William!**
The Wisest Worm in the World!
Rose Impey and Shoo Rayner

1 84121 256 3

Precious **Potter**
The Heaviest Cat in the World!
Rose Impey and Shoo Rayner

1 84121 236 9

A Birthday for **Bluebell**
The Oldest Cow in the World!
Rose Impey and Shoo Rayner

1 84121 228 8

A Fortune for **Yo-Yo**
The Richest Dog in the World!
Rose Impey and Shoo Rayner

1 84121 230 X

Phew, Sidney!
The Sweetest-Smelling Skunk in the World!
Rose Impey and Shoo Rayner

1 84121 234 2

1 84121 248 2

1 84121 242 3

1 84121 232 6

1 84121 246 6

1 84121 258 X

1 84121 250 4

1 84121 254 7

Read all the Colour CRACKERS books!

Collect all the
Colour Crackers!